The Lipgloss Queen
Kingdom Kid Affirmations

Written By Jennifer L. Sargent

Illustrated By Ananta Mohanta

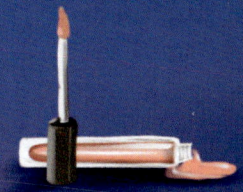

The Lip Gloss Queen: Kingdom Kid Affirmations
(The Princess Edition)
Copyright © 2023 by The Pretty Little Writing Boutique, LLC.
All rights reserved.
No portion of this book may be reproduced or distributed in any form without permission from the publisher. For permission to use materials from this book outside of purposes of reviewal, please contact the publishing company.
This work and all characters in this book are fictitious. Any resemblance to any real persons, living or not living, is purely coincidental.

The Pretty Little Writing Boutique, LLC.
P.O. Box 367
Whiting, IN 46394
prettypublishingboutique@gmail.com
prettypublishingboutique.com

Author: Jennifer L. Sargent
Illustrator: Ananta Mohanta

ISBN # 979-8-9856070-5-5

Series Book Number: 2

kingdomkidaffirmations.com

To all my Lip Gloss Queens,

Dream big and let nothing stand in your way! You can be and do anything you set your mind to! Always remember to wear your lip gloss and say your affirmations. Speak it, believe it, and you will receive it! And may your lip gloss allow your best qualities to shine from within, radiating your beauty to the world.

To my big brother, Thel Sargent Jr., Bobbie, and Boykin Gradford,

Special appreciation goes to you for reminding me of who I am and who I can become. Thanks for always being there and supporting me wholeheartedly. Your words of encouragement mean the world to me.

From My Heart to Yours,

Jennifer L. Sargent

beautiful
powerful
unique
smart
creative
kind
capable
determined
winner
friendly

It was a Saturday morning, and Kamia Johnson stood in front of the mirror, speaking her daily affirmations.
"I am smart. I am determined. I am capable. I believe in me! I am all that God says I am!"
Her big sister Kayla called out, "Kamiaaaa! It's time to go!" Kamia quickly joined her sister, and they headed out the door for a trip to the mall.

"Would you like to try some on?" asked Carla, the clerk.
Kamia happily accepted the offer and tried on each lip gloss, finally settling on the watermelon and peach flavors.

"Come on, lip gloss queen, I'm running late for my hair appointment," Kayla called out to Kamia, and they hurriedly left the store, thanking Ms. Carla.

The next night, Kamia had a special dream and an angel named Brenda appeared to her.

"Child of God, your heavenly father loves you dearly and has big plans for you! You have the power to be all that you desire. So, dream girl, dream, you can do anything, you're the lip gloss queen!" Angel Brenda announced.

On Monday morning, Kamia woke up feeling empowered. Before heading to school, she put on some of her new

lip gloss and, just like every morning, she stood in front of her mirror and said her daily affirmations. "I am smart. I am determined. I am capable. I believe in me! I am all that God says I am!"

She then smiled at herself in the mirror and headed to school.

Courageous

"Good morning, class," greeted Ms. J.
"Who knows what time it is?" asked Ms. J.
"It's affirmation time!" the kids yelled out with excitement.
"What time is it?" Ms. J. asked again.
"Affirmation time!" the kids yelled even louder!
After the kids had said their daily affirmations, Ms. J. reminded them of the big science fair on Thursday. Science was Kamia's favorite subject. Although excited, she had no idea what she wanted to do for her science project.

After class, while in the girls' bathroom, as Kamia put on some more of her watermelon lip gloss, she saw a new girl looking very sad. "Hi, my name is Kamia. Are you okay?" "I'm Remy," the girl said. "I just wish I had better clothes so the other girls would not laugh at me."

"Awww, I'm sorry," said Kamia. "But maybe if you try some of my new lip gloss, it will make you feel better." She pulled out the peach lip gloss and handed it to Remy. "Now repeat after me," said Kamia. "I am creative. I am unique. I love my clothes and the way I look. I believe in me! I am all that God says I am."

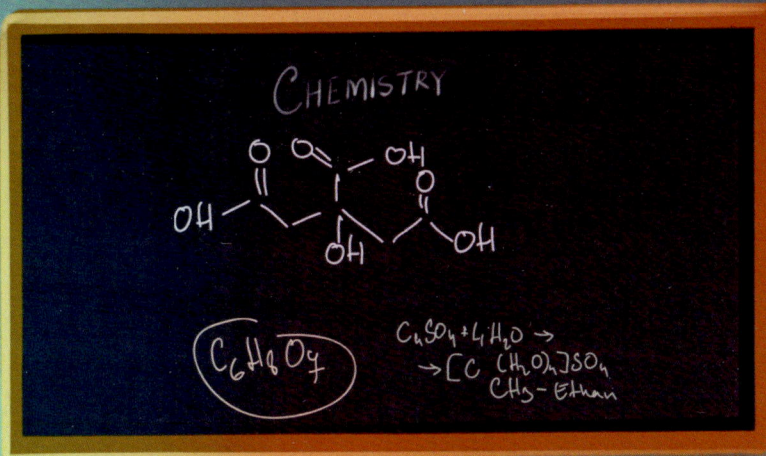

Kamia ran all the way to her Aunt Dotty's lab. She told her Aunt Dotty all about her dream, the science fair, and her new friend Remy. "Aunt Dotty, will you help me?" asked Kamia.
"Of course, I will," replied Aunt Dotty. They got to work and spent the rest of the day mixing up ingredients until they came up with the perfect mixtures and flavors of lip gloss.
"Let's go, lip gloss queen, it's past your bedtime, and we've got to get you home," Aunt Dotty told Kamia.
"Thanks for your help, Aunt Dotty. I wonder why everyone keeps calling me the lip gloss queen," said Kamia. Aunt Dotty just looked at her niece and smiled.

That night Kamia went home feeling excited about the science fair. She took a beautiful mirror out of a little trunk by her bed that her grandmother had given her a few years ago before she went to heaven.

Before she went to bed, Kamia prayed to God that she would become one of the winners at the science fair on Thursday. Although she could not see Brenda the angel, she was standing right next to Kamia praying for her. Kamia could hear Brenda's soft, sweet voice saying those words again. "Dream girl, dream, you can do anything; you're the lip gloss queen." As Kamia continued to pray, God heard her prayers. God opened up the heavens and sprinkled heavenly gold dust all over Kamia and a cloud of glory rested over her.

It was the day of the science fair; all eyes were on Kamia as the kids presented their science projects one by one. When it was Kamia's turn, she allowed all the girls to test out the different flavors of lip gloss and look in her grandmother's mirror as they spoke positive words over themselves.

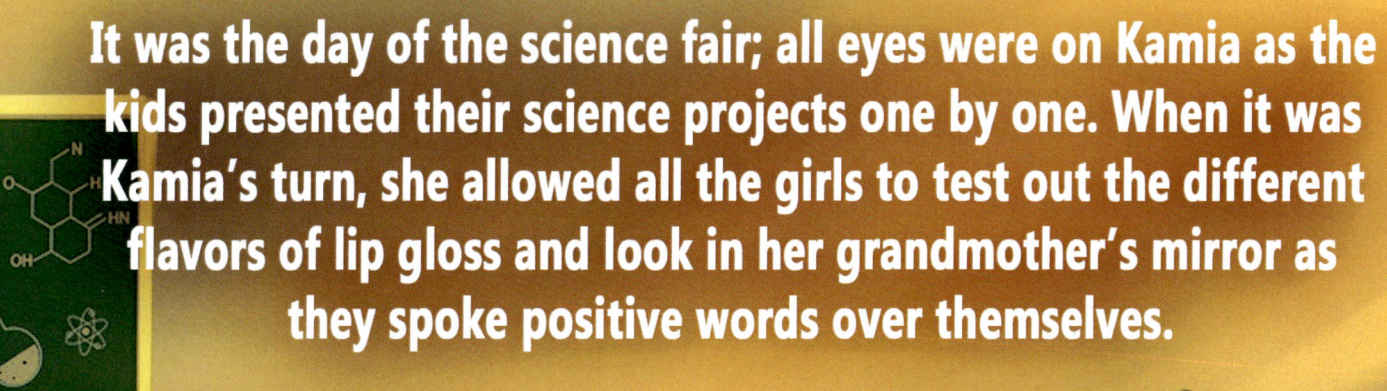

Kamia's project wowed the crowd. They did not know that it was God's power working through Kamia and her project. Using her lip gloss and mirror, the girls felt empowered and confident. Kamia won first place and even considered starting her own lip gloss business.

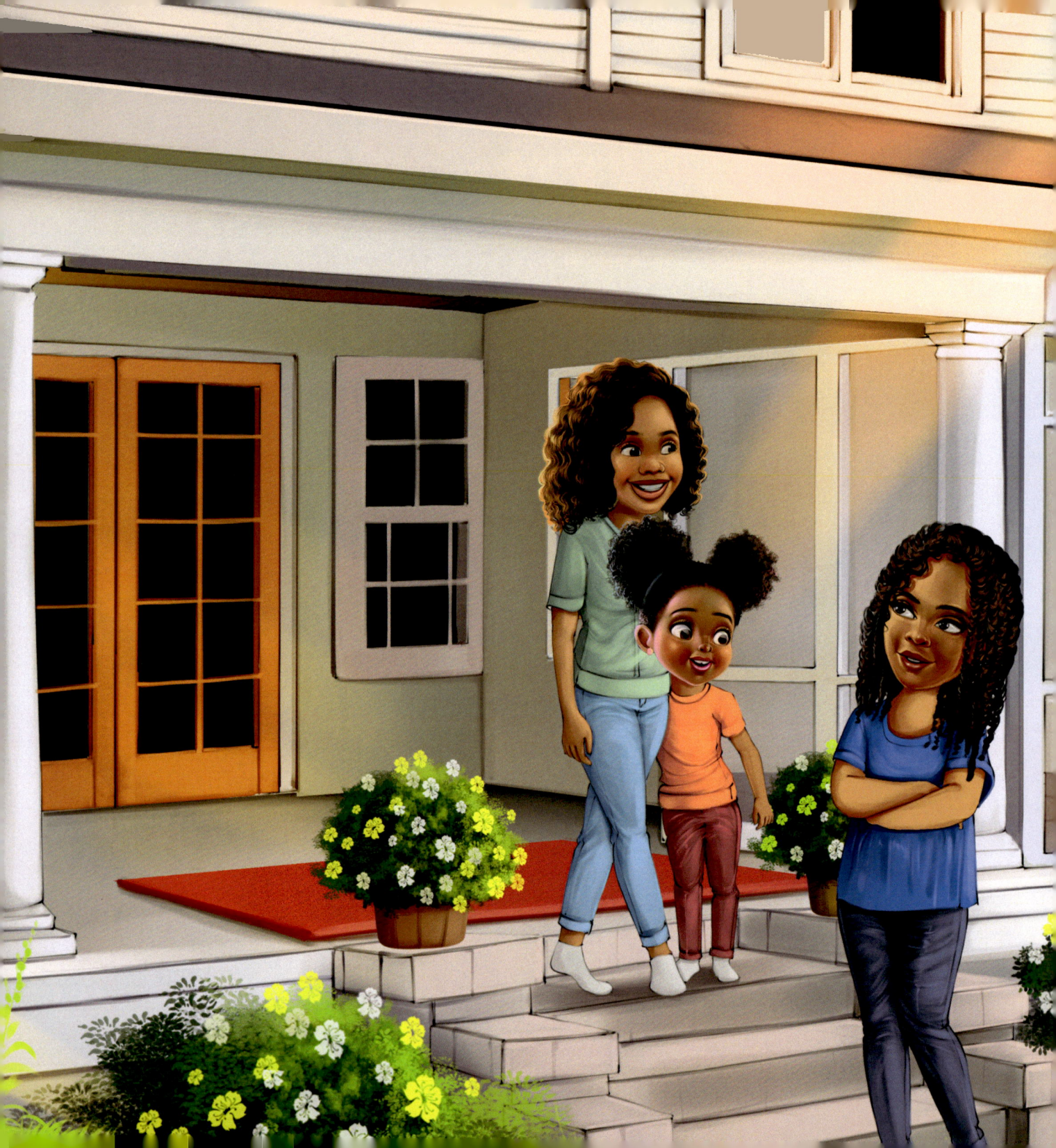

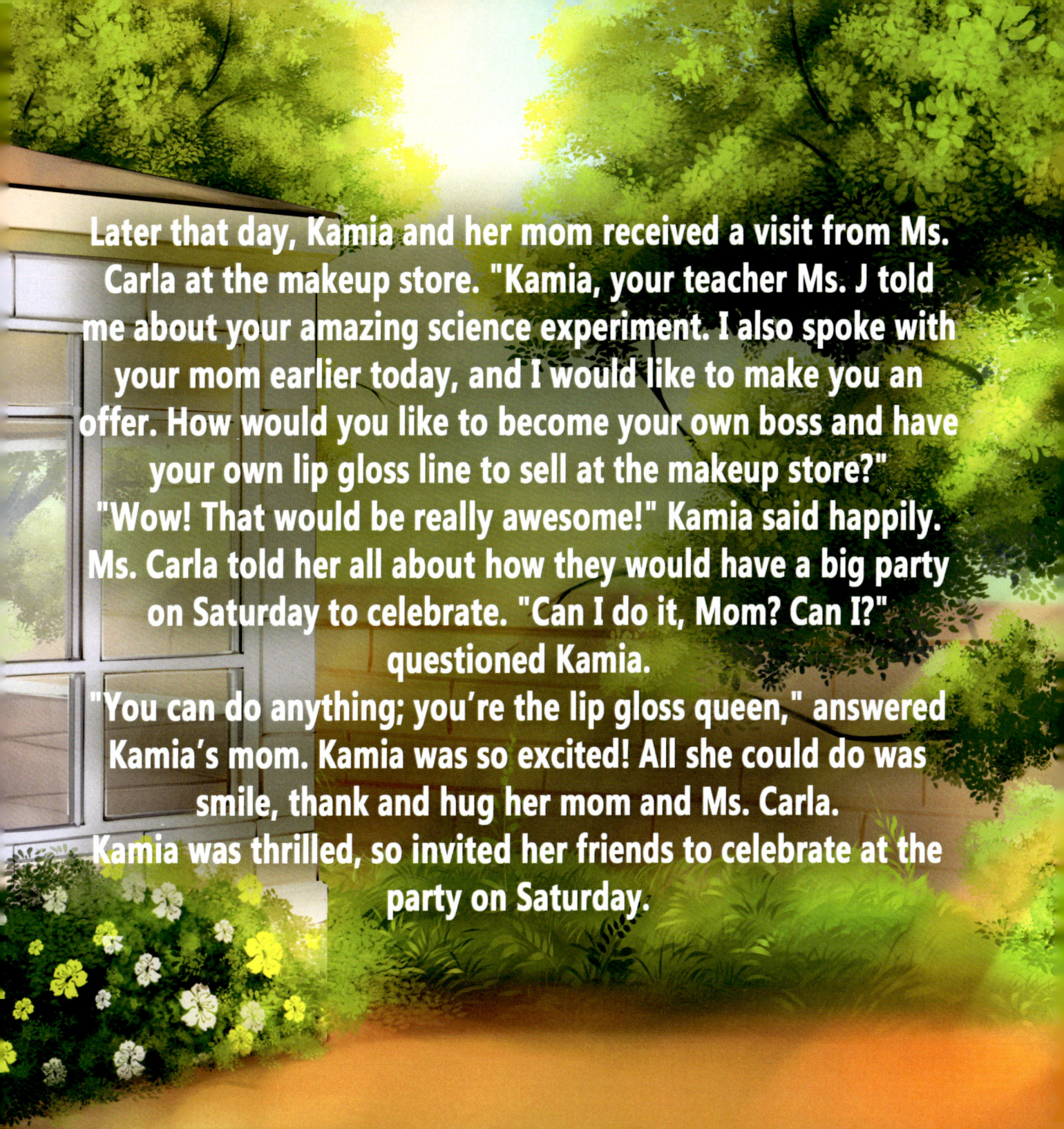

Later that day, Kamia and her mom received a visit from Ms. Carla at the makeup store. "Kamia, your teacher Ms. J told me about your amazing science experiment. I also spoke with your mom earlier today, and I would like to make you an offer. How would you like to become your own boss and have your own lip gloss line to sell at the makeup store?"
"Wow! That would be really awesome!" Kamia said happily. Ms. Carla told her all about how they would have a big party on Saturday to celebrate. "Can I do it, Mom? Can I?" questioned Kamia.
"You can do anything; you're the lip gloss queen," answered Kamia's mom. Kamia was so excited! All she could do was smile, thank and hug her mom and Ms. Carla.
Kamia was thrilled, so invited her friends to celebrate at the party on Saturday.

The next day when Kamia arrived at school, there was a long line of kids waiting at her locker to place an order for her new lip gloss. Even the boys placed orders for their sisters. Kamia was so excited! She could not wait for her big day tomorrow.

It was finally Kamia's big day! The makeup store was packed! So many kids showed up to celebrate Kamia and her new lip gloss business. She was so excited and could not believe all this was happening. She heard those special words again that day, "dream girl, dream, you can do anything! You're the lip gloss queen!"

And because Kamia believed that she was smart, capable, and she was always determined, God blessed Kamia with all that her heart desired and more! From then on, she was called the "lip gloss queen."

Jennifer L. Sargent

Author . Speaker . Entrepreneur

🌐 kingdomkidaffirmations.com

✉️ kingdomkidsaffirmations@gmail.com

📘 Jennifer L. Sargent

👥 Kingdom Kid Affirmations

📷 _thecrownedjewel_

Affirmation and Book Coach